Success S

Earl Goodale

Alpha Editions

This edition published in 2024

ISBN : 9789364733946

Design and Setting By
Alpha Editions
www.alphaedis.com
Email - info@alphaedis.com

SUCCESS STORY

By EARL GOODALE

*Terra resounded to the triple toast of the
Haldorian hordes: For Haldor! For Glory!
And for Heaven's sake, let us out of here!*

Once my name was Ameet Ruxt, my skin was light blue, and I was a moderately low-ranking member of the Haldorian Empire. Or should I say I was a member of the lower income group? No, definitely "low-ranking," because in a warrior society, even one with as high a technological level as a statistician sits low on the totem pole. He is handed the wrong end of the stick—call it what you will; he's the one who doesn't acquire even one wife for years and he hasn't a courtesy title. He's the man they draft into their Invasion Forces—the Haldorians are always invading someone—and turn him into a Fighter Basic in a third of a year.

"Look," I'd complained to the burly two-striper in the Receiving Center, "I'm a trained statistician with a degree and...."

"Say Sir, when you address me."

I started over again. "I know, Sir, that they use statisticians in the service. So if Haldor needs me in the service it's only sensible that I should work in statistics."

The Hweetoral looked bored, but I've found out since that all two-stripers looked bored; it's because so many of them have attained, at that rank, their life's ambition. "Sure, sure. But we just got a directive down on all you paper-pushers. Every one of you from now on out is headed for Fighter Basic Course. You know, I envy you, Ruxt. Haldor, what I wouldn't give to be out there with real men again! Jetting down on some new planet—raying down the mongrels till they yelled for mercy—and grabbing a new chunk of sky for the Empire. Haldor! That's the life!" He glanced modestly down at his medalled chest.

"Yes, Sir," I said, "it sure is. But look at my examination records you have right there. Physically I'm only a 3 and you have to have a 5 to go to Basic Fighter. And besides," I threw in the clincher, though I was a bit ashamed of it, "my fighting aptitude only measures a 2!"

The Hweetoral sneered unsubtly and grabbed a scriber with heavy fingers. A couple of slashes, a couple of new entries, and lo, I was now a 5 in both departments. I was qualified in every respect.

"See," he said, "that's your first lesson in the Service, Ruxt. Figures don't mean a thing, because they can always be changed. That's something a figure pusher like you has to learn. So—" he shoved out that ponderous hand and crushed mine before I could protect myself—"good luck, Ruxt. I know you'll get through that course—alive, I mean." He chuckled heartily. "And I know men!"

He was right. I got through alive. But then, 76.5 per cent of draftees do get through the Basic Fighter Course, alive. But for me it took a drastic rearrangement of philosophy.

Me, all I'd ever wanted was a good life. An adequate income, art and music, congenial friends, an understanding wife—just one wife was all I'd ever hoped for. As you can see, I was an untypical Haldorian on every point.

After my first day in Basic Fighter Course I just wanted to stay alive.

"There's two kinds of men we turn out here," our Haldor told us as we lined up awkwardly for the first time (that scene so loved by vision-makers). We new draftees called our Trontar our Haldor because he actually had the power over our bodies that the chaplains assured us the Heavenly Haldor had over our liberated spirits. Our Trontar looked us over with his fatherly stare, flexing his powerful arm muscles so that his three tattooed stripes rippled and danced. "Yeah," he went on, "two kinds of men: Fighting men and dead men!" The Trontar grinned that fighting Haldorian grin you see all your lives on the Prop Sheets. "And I'll tell you something, men. When you leave here—all Fighters Basic—I'm going to envy you. Yeah, I'll really envy you gutsy killers when you go out in that big Out-There and grab yourselves a new chunk of sky." He paused and studied our faces. "Now we're gonna run, and I do mean run, two full decades. The last four men in get to do it over again, and pull kitchen duty tonight too."

I tried, as others have tried, to slip quietly out of Basic Fighter. I tried being sick, but following sick report one found oneself doing a full day's training—after the understanding medics had shoved some pep pills into you. I demanded a physical examination. They weren't going to push me around.

After a couple of days in solitary, I asked in a nice way for physical evaluation.

Well, I asked. I wasn't very smart in those days.

They weren't interested in my story of how my records had been falsified or in my fighting aptitude.

"Look, draftee," the psycho-man said after I finally got to him, "the fact that you've got to see me shows you have enough of a fighting aptitude. Your Trontar didn't encourage you to request evaluation, did he? And he isn't going to like you very much when you report back to your platoon, is he?"

I shuddered. "Not exactly."

"Call me Sir."

"No, Sir. But I was desperate, Sir. I don't think I can stand...."

"Draftee, you know that some unfortunate men break down in training and that we have to take them out. Maybe you've already lost some that way. Suppose you were brought in here, gibbering, yowling, and drooling—I guess we'd have to cure you and send you back home as non-fighter material, eh?"

Someone up here liked me! Here was a tip on how to escape back to the old quiet life. I nodded agreeably.

"But you know, don't you," he said softly, "that first we run a thorough test on our drooling draftee? Say it's you...."

I nodded again.

"We most always detect fakers. And you know there's a death penalty for any Haldorian attempting to escape his duty." He smiled sadly, and reminiscently.

I nodded. Maybe someone up here didn't like me.

"So we'd shoot you dead with one of those primitive projectile weapons, as an object lesson for both you and the draftees we had remaining."

I nodded and tried to show by my countenance how much I approved of people being shot dead with primitive weapons.

"But suppose," he went on, "that you'd really cracked up or that you'd faked successfully?"

"Yes, Sir?" Hope returned, hesitantly and on tip-toes, ready to flee.

"Then we'd cure you," he said. "But the cure unfortunately involves the destruction of your higher mental faculties. And so there'd be nothing for it but to ship you off to one of the mining planets. That's standard procedure, if you didn't know. But I think you'll be all right now, don't you?"

Hope fled. I assured him that I'd be just fine and reported back, on the double, to my training platoon.

"Just in time, Ruxt," my Trontar greeted me. "Back for full duty, I take it? That's the Haldorian spirit!" He turned to the platoon which was lined up like three rows of sweaty statues. "Men, remember what I told you about taking cover when you're under fire—and staying under cover? Just suppose we suddenly came under fire—flat trajectory stuff—out here on this flat exercise ground with no cover except in that latrine pit over there. Would any of you hesitate to dive into that latrine pit? And once in there, safe and sound, would any of you not stay there until I gave the word to come out?"

A perceptible shudder passed like a wave over the platoon. We knew the Trontar did not ask pointless questions.

"Of course you wouldn't," he assured us, "and you'd even stay in there all day under this hot sun if you had to. Ruxt! You're rested and refreshed from visiting the hospital. You demonstrate how it's done."

It was a long day, even though my Trontar kindly sent some sandwiches over to me at high noon. I didn't eat much. But I did do a lot of thinking.

There was one last hope. I wrote a letter to a remote clan relative who was supposed to have a small amount of influence.

It was a moving letter. I told how my test results had been falsified, what beasts our trainers were, how the medics refused to retest me—very much the standard letter that new Haldorian trainees write. As I went out to mail this plea, one evening, I met two of my fellow trainees starting out on a night march in full field equipment.

"How come?" I asked, instantly fearful that I'd missed some notice on the bulletin board.

"We wrote letters," one of them said simply.

"The Trontar censors all our mail," said the other. "Didn't you know? Oh, well, neither did we."

As they marched off, I made a small bonfire out of my letter after first, almost, just throwing it away—before I remembered that the Hweetorals checked our waste cans. What a man has to do to hold two measly stripes!

Acceptance of the inevitable is the beginning of wisdom, says the ancient Haldorian sage. I put in an application for transfer to the Statistical Services to be effective upon *completion* of Basic Fighter Course.

"Statistical Services?" the Company Clerk asked. "What's that? Anyhow, you're going to be a Fighter Basic, if you get through this training," he said darkly. The Company Clerk was a sad victim of our Haldorian passion for realistic training; he had lacked one day of completing Fighter Basic when he'd let his leg dangle a bit too long after he'd scaled a wall, and the training gentlemen had unemotionally shot it off. As it turned out, our efficient surgeon/replacers had been unable, for some technical reason, to grow back enough leg for full duty. So there was nothing for it but to use the man as could be best done. They'd made him a clerk—mainly because that was the specialty they were shortest of at the time.

"Who says you can put in for Statistical Services?" the Company Clerk demanded.

"Reg 39-47A." I was learning my way around. The night before I was on orderly duty in the office. I had tracked down the chapter and verse which, theoretically, allowed a man to change his destiny.

"Know the Regs, do you? Starting to be a trouble-maker, huh? Yeah, Ruxt, I'll put in your application."

I turned away with some feeling of relief. This might possibly work.

The Company Clerk called me back. "You know the Regs so good, Ruxt," he said. "How come you didn't ask me for permission to leave? I'm cadre, you know." He leaned back in his chair and grinned at me. "Just to help you remember the correct Haldorian deportment I'm putting you on kitchen duty for the next three nights. That way," he grinned again, "you can divide up your five hours of sleep over three nights instead of crowding them all into one."

Poor deluded Company Clerk! I actually averaged three hours of sleep every one of those three nights—after I found out that the mess Trontar would accept my smoking ration.

I felt that I was beginning to understand the system, a little and at long last, particularly after I saw my co-workers in the kitchen doing what should have been my work.

II

Then we started combat training, and then we started losing our normal 23.5 per cent.

It wasn't too bad as long as they stuck to the primitive stuff. I mean, you can see arrows and spears coming at you, and even if you have had only the five hours of sleep you can either duck the projectiles or catch them on your shield. And with the medics on the alert, the wounds are painful but seldom fatal. You just end up with a week's hospitalization and slip back to the next training group. But when they go up to the explosively-propelled solids, when the Trontar smirks and says: "Men, this is called a boomer, or a banger, or maybe sometimes a firestick, depending on what planet you're fighting on," and when he holds up a contraption of wood and metal with a hole at one end and a handle on the other—then, Draftee, look out!

It takes time to learn. It isn't till you associate a bang in the distance with a perforated man beside you that you do learn. And when you finally come under fire from our regular production weapons like rays—well!

You might wonder why they run us through the entire history of weapons starting with the sling and ending with the slithers—the name servicemen give to those Zeta Rays that diverge from line of sight to drop in on a dug-in enemy. The usual explanation is that Haldorians are still invading places where the natives still use such things as bows and arrows. But I think, myself, that it's something the Mil Prop guys figured out. The idea is, as I see it, to run you right through the whole course of our fighting, invading Haldorian history, and in that way to make a better fighter out of you. And you do get rid of the death-prones before there's much time or work invested in them—or before their inevitable early death means the failure of a mission. Haldoria—most practical of Empires!

But they didn't make a fighter of me. All they did was to reinforce my natural survival instinct considerably, acquaint me with the tortuous ways of the service, and give me a great urge for a peaceful existence. But to all appearances, as I stood in the orderly room after graduation, I was the ideal poster-picture of a Haldorian, completely uniformed with polished power boots and rayer, a crawler to the higher-ups and a stomper on the lower-downs, a Fighter Basic with no compassion but with a certified aptitude for advancement to at least the rank of Trontar.

"Fighter Basic Ruxt," the Dispositions Hweetoral announced.

"Here, Sir!"

"Your application for transfer to Statistical Services has been disapproved."
The two-striper's expression showed what he, as a fighting man, thought of
the Statistical Services. "But we've got a real assignment for you, Ruxt! The
27th Invasion Force is all set to drop on a new system. You're lucky, Ruxt,
that you put in that application. We had to hold you till it bounced. Your
buddies got shipped to those rear-echelon guard outfits, but you're going to
a real fighting one. It should be a good invasion—this new system's got
atomic fission, I hear. And I'd like to tell you something, Ruxt...."

"I know what, Sir," I said. "You envy me."

The 27th was a real fighting unit all right: they had their own neckerchief,
their own war cry, and a general who was on his way up. Now they had me.

And they were going to get another system for the Haldorian Empire.

You see, those intelligent worms, or maybe they are slugs—I'm a bit vague
on universe geography—over on the next Galaxy but one, give us
Haldorians all sorts of difficulties. They insist on freedom, self-
determination, and all that sort of thing. That's all very well, but they insist
on them for themselves. Our high-level planners decided that another solar
system would make a better offensive set-up for Haldoria. The planners, I
understand, have all sorts of esoteric theories about the ideal shape and size
of an offensive unit. They ring in time and something related to time which
makes Galaxy distances differ according to which direction you are
travelling. As I say, esoteric.

The only thing that mattered to me was that some technicians had fed
some data into a computer and it had hiccuped and said: "You'll need
such-and-such a planet to control such-and-such a solar system, and that
will give you a better offensive set-up." Then the computer hiccuped again
and said: "You'll need to draft and train Ameet Ruxt to help on this little
job of taking over this planet called Terra, or Earth."

That's what it amounted to, anyhow. Consequently I joined the 27th
Invasion Force.

"So you've got an application in for transfer to the Statistical Services,
huh?" Trontar Hytd, my new platoon three-striper, asked when I reported
in for duty with the 27th.

"Yes, Sir." I'd learned, along the line, that one should never give up when
applying for a transfer—just keep one in the mill.

"Huh, Borr, this new guy likes to work with figures," Trontar Hytd growled at Hweetoral Borr, my new squad leader. "Thinks he doesn't want to be a Fighter." Trontar Hytd looked at me questioningly.

I didn't say anything. I'd learned a lot in Basic Fighter Course.

"Figures?" asked Hweetoral Borr. I could see a train of thought had been started in the Hweetoral's mind.

"Yeah, figures," snapped Trontar Hytd. "He likes to count things, Borr. Get it?"

"Guess we need all our ray charges counted, for one thing," suggested Hweetoral Borr. "I get all mixed up with them figures."

"After training hours, of course," Trontar Hytd said.

"Of course, Trontar. And someone's gotta jawbone some kind of report on ammo expenditures every training day. Maybe after the rest of us have sacked in, for instance?"

"Of course. Okay, Hweetoral, I guess you got the idea."

Invasion was almost a relief after that brief bit of refresher training the 27th was going through.

Our General-on-the-way-up had outlined his plan of attack: "Drop'm, hit'm, lift'm and drop'm again." So I dropped, hit the defenders, was lifted to a new center of resistance, and dropped again. I understand it was a standard type of invasion, there's only one way to do simple things.

Once in a while, these days, I remember those sadistic and battle-hardened comrades of mine. Hard, gutsy Trontar Hytd stayed on his feet to direct his platoon underground after our Kansas force collapsed, and one of those little fission weapons separated his body parts too widely for even our unsentimentally competent surgeon/replacer to reassemble him. Well, they had a go at the job, but they had to ray down what they created—some primitive regression had set in and the creature was hungry.

And rough and tough Hweetoral Borr incautiously scratched his hairy ear just when one of those rude projectile weapons was firing at him. The slug slipped through that opening the Hweetoral had made in his body armor. With the brain gone—or such brain as Hweetoral Borr possessed—our kindly old surgeon/replacer was foxed again.

Then there were the new germs....

But these things are as nothing to the creative military mind. A swarm of regulations, manuals and directives issue forth from headquarters, and force fields cease to collapse, and fighters keep their body armor on and adjusted. When something like the influenza germ wipes out half a platoon, the wheels turn, a new vaccine is devised, and no more Haldorians die from that particular germ. All the individual has to do is to live from one injection to the next (any civilized enemy always dreams up new diseases), move from one enemy strong point to the next, and dream of the day when he can return to his old life. For me it was a dream of returning to that quiet tiny room with its walls lined with the best of Haldorian art—just cheap reproductions, of course—and never again to handle a rayer or to wear armor. Real life, meanwhile, went on.

"Fighter First-Class Ruxt! Take these men and blast that strong point!" That would be the order somewhere in Missouri, or maybe in Mississippi— I never was much good on micro-geography. "Hweetoral Ruxt! Take your squad and clean out that city. New Orleans they call it. Get their formal surrender and make damn sure there are no guerrillas left when the colonel comes through to inspect."

By the time I was Trontar Ruxt the invasion was practically over. As I say, it was the standard thing with one or two countries holding out after all hope was gone—England never did formally surrender, not that it mattered—and our successful General was made a Sub-Marshal of the Haldorian Empire.

A real promotion and a great honor. Much good it did him when he ventured his battle fleet too far into the Slug lines a year later.

With the fighting over—the real fighting, I mean—the ever-efficient Haldorians started moving their troops off Earth to get ready for a new and bigger invasion that the computers had decreed. Only a few troops were to be left behind for occupation and guard stuff.

I had a talk with a fat Assignments Trontar in his plush office.

"You know, Trontar," I said, "I was hoping to see more of this world here, and the rumor is that all of us excess combat types are being shipped to a training world to be shaped into new invasion forces."

"Tough," he said. He should know. He'd requisitioned a mansion complete with servants and everything. He even had a native trained to drive one of their luxuriously inefficient ground vehicles. What a deal! That Trontar had no worries, *his* anti-grav ray was working.

"I heard that a man doesn't even need any money if he's stationed down at our headquarters," I said, and I hauled out a handful of Haldorian notes from my pocket. "Guess I wouldn't need this stuff if I was transferred down to our headquarters."

"Who needs money?" he asked. "Guys all the time trying to bribe me, Trontar. You'd be surprised. Sure glad you aren't, though, because I do hate to turn anyone in."

I put the money back in my pocket. "Speaking of turning in people," I said casually, "you ever have any trouble with the undercover boys about all this loot you've picked up?" This, I thought, would shake him—and at the same time I marvelled at how I'd changed from a simple, naive statistician to a tough and conniving combat NCO.

He yawned all over his fat face and swung his swivel chair so that he could better admire the picture beside his desk. I recognized the picture as a moderately good reproduction of a Huxtner, a minor painter of our XXVth. "No," the Assignments Trontar said, "it turns out that one of my sept brothers runs the local watch birds. He often drops in here to visit with me. But anything I can do for you, Trontar?"

"No," I said, and I fired at the only possible loophole left, "I'll just leave quietly so you can admire your Huxtner."

He swung back to me with a start. "You recognize a Huxtner? You're the first man I've ever met in the service who ever heard of Huxtner, let alone recognizing one of his masterpieces! Hey, did you know I brought this all the way from home in my hammock roll? And just look at the coloring of that figure there!"

The loophole had been blasted wide open. "You're lucky," I said, and I went on to lie about how I'd lost my own Huxtner prints in the invasion. "No one," I continued, "ever got quite that flesh tint of Huxtner's, did they?"

Huxtner, by the way, is notorious for using a yellow undercoat for his blue flesh colors, unlike every realistic painter before or after who have all used green undercoats—what else? Imagine a chrome-yellow underlaying a blue skin color. All Huxtner's figures look like two-week corpses—but Huxtner enthusiasts are unique.

The Assignments Trontar and I had a nice long chat about Huxtner, at the conclusion of which he insisted on scratching my name from the list of combat-bound men and putting me on a much smaller list of men scheduled for our guard outfit, stationed at the old Terran capital of Washington.

I had an un-Haldorian feeling of having arranged my own life after that incident. That feeling persisted even after I took over one of the guard platoons and discovered that life in a guard outfit is rather similar to Basic Fighter Course.

"Trontar Ruxt! Two men of your platoon have tarnished armor. Get them working on it, and maybe you'd better stay and see that they do it properly."

"Yes, Sir."

One lives and learns. I turned the job of supervising the armor cleaning to the Hweetorals of the squads and then I went home to my native woman. Yes, this guard's outfit life was like Fighter Basic Course.

But only for the lower ranks.

III

Life wasn't too unendurable in those days. The duties were incredibly dull, of course, but the danger of sudden death had receded, since only a few fanatics still tried to pick off us occupation troops. And this new world of Haldoria's was rich in the things a sensitive and artistic man appreciates: painting, sculpture, music. Then there was this new and pleasing thing of living with a woman....

But it wouldn't last long.

Soon there'd be another planet to invade and maybe a space battle with the great enemy. More years of cramped living and lurking danger, for in the Empire one was drafted for the duration, and this duration was now some four hundred years old. The most Trontar Ruxt could expect, the very most, was to somehow keep alive for another fifty years and then to retire on a small pension to one of the lesser worlds of the Empire.

"Trontar Ruxt! Your records show that you're a statistician." My commanding officer stared at me suspiciously, for a fighting man, even one on guard duty, distrusts office personnel. And as everyone knows, "Once a fighting man, always a fighting man." I think my C.O.'s last action had been thirty years ago.

"I was a statistician before I got in the service, Sir."

"Well, they're screaming over at headquarters for qualified office personnel, and we have to send them any trained men we have—of any rank."

"It's for Haldor, Sir," I said. By now I knew the correct answer was most often the noncommittal one.

I reported to the Headquarters, 27th Invasion Force. The rumor was that Phase II, Reduction of Inhabitants to Slavery with Shipment to Haldorian Colonies, was about to start. And also, our Planners were supposed to be well into Phase III, Terraforming, already. Terraforming was necessary, of course, to bring the average temperature of earth down to something like the sub-arctic so that we Haldorians could live here in comfort. We lost quite a few fighters during invasion when their cooling systems broke down. Rumor, as always, was dead right; and the Headquarters was a mad rat-race.

The Senior Trontar of the office was delighted to get another body.

"Took your time getting here, Ruxt! You guard louts don't know the meaning of time, do you?"

I remained at attention.

"So you're a statistician, are you? Well, we don't need any statisticians now. We just got in a whole squad of them. Can you use a writer, maybe?"

"Yes, Sir," I did not remind the Senior Trontar that using a writer was a clerk's job, not a Trontar's, not a combat three-striper's, because the chances were that he knew it, for one thing. And he could easily make me a clerk, for another thing.

"Okay. Now that we understand each other," the Senior Trontar grinned, "or that you understand me, which is all that matters, here's your job." He handed me a stack of scribbled notes, some rolls of speech tape and a couple of cans of visual stuff. "Make up a report in standard format like this example. Consolidate all this stuff into it. This report has to be ready in two days, and it has to be perfect. No misspellings, no erasures, no nothing. Got that?"

"Yes, Sir."

"Yes, Sir," he mimicked. "Haldor only knows why they couldn't send me a few clerks instead of a squad of statisticians and one guard Trontar. Do you know what this stuff is that you're going to work up? It's the final report on our invasion here!"

I looked impressed. Strange how you learn, after a while, even the facial expression you are supposed to wear.

"Do you know why this report has to be perfect in format and appearance?" I wouldn't say the Senior Trontar's manner was bullying, quite. Perhaps one could call it hectoring. "Because the Accountant is out in this sector somewhere and we have to be ready for him if he drops in."

This time I didn't have to try to look impressed. The Accountant is the man who passes judgment on the conduct of all military matters—though of course he's not one man, but maybe a dozen of them. Armed with the invaluable weapon of hindsight, he drops in after an invasion is completed. He determines whether the affair has gone according to regulations, or whether there has been carelessness, slackness or wasting of Haldorian resources of men or material. Additionally he monitors civil administration of colonies and federated worlds. There are stories of Generals becoming Fighter Basics and Chief Administrators becoming sub-clerks after an Accountant's visit.

I got the report done, but it took the full two days—mainly because fighting men make such incomplete and erroneous reports while action is going on. I got to understand the exasperated concern of office personnel who have to consolidate varied fragments into a coherent whole. And adding to the natural difficulties of the task was the continual presence of the Senior Trontar, and his barbed comments and lurid promises as to what would follow my failure at the work.

But the report was done and sent in to the Adjutant.

It came back covered with scribbled changes, additions, and deletions—and it came back carried by a much disturbed Senior Trontar.

"Who in Haldor do they think I am?" he moaned. "I just handed on to you the figures that they gave me. Me! And threatening me with duty on a space freighter ... and one into the Slug area at that!"

I thought, as I looked at my ruined script, that guard duty wasn't so bad, and that even combat wasn't rough *all* the time.

"See, Trontar," the four-striper said, calling me by my proper rank for the first time, "you did a good job, the Adjutant himself said so. But these figures...." he shuddered. "If the Accountant should see these we'd all be for it. Space-freighter duty would be getting off light." The Senior Trontar seemed almost human to me right then.

"I just put down what you gave me," I said.

"Yeah, sure, Ruxt. But I didn't realize, nobody realized, how bad the figures were till they were all together and written up. Look, this report shows that we shouldn't Terraform this planet—that we can't make a nudnick on the slavery proposition—and that maybe we shouldn't have even invaded this inferno at all."

"So what do you want me to do?"

"I'll tell you what you're going to do...." The Senior Trontar had regained his normal nasty disposition. "You're going to re-do this report. You're going to re-do it starting now, you're going to work on it all night, and you're going to have it on my desk and in perfect shape when I come in in the morning, or, by Haldor, the next thing you write will be your transfer to the space freighter run nearest the Slug Galaxy." The Senior Trontar ran momentarily out of breath. "And," he came back strongly, "you won't be going as no Trontar, neither!"

"It'll be on your desk in the morning, Sir," I said.

Deck hands on the space freighter run were, I'd heard, particularly expendable.

By the middle of the third watch I had completed a perfect copy of the report complete with attachments, appendices, and supplements. And also by this time I knew from the differences between the original report and this jawboned version that someone had goofed badly in undertaking this invasion, and then had goofed worse in not calling the thing off. Now there was to be considerable covering-up of tracks. The thought suddenly came to me that a guard's trontar named Ruxt knew rather a lot of what had gone on. Following that mildly worrying thought came a notion that perhaps a guard's trontar named Ruxt might be considered by some as just another set of tracks to be covered up. That far-off retirement on a small but steady income became even more unlikely, and the possibilities began to appear of a quick end in the Slug-shattered hulk of a space freighter.

Had the Senior Trontar changed in his attitude towards me, towards the end of the day, perhaps acted as though I were a condemned man? Possibly. And had some of the officers been whispering about me late in the afternoon? Could have been.

Shaken, I wandered down to the mess hall and joined a group of third-watch guards, who were goofing off while their Trontar was checking more distant guard posts.

"It's easy," one of them was telling the others. "All you got to do is to slip some surgeon/replacer a few big notes and he gives you this operation which makes you look like a native. And then you just settle down on Astarte for the rest of your life with the women just begging you to let them support you."

"You mean you'd rather live on some lousy federated world than be a Haldorian in the Invasion Forces?" There was a strong sardonic note in the questioner's voice.

"Man, you ever been on Astarte?" the first man asked incredulously.

"Yeah, but how are you going to be sure that the surgeon/replacer doesn't turn you in?" objected one of the others. "He could take your money, do the operation, and have you picked up. That way he'd have the money and get a medal too."

"I'd get around that," the talky guy said, "I'd just...."

At this point he was jabbed in the arm by one of his buddies who had noticed my eavesdropping. The man shut up. All four of them drifted off to their posts.

I went reluctantly back to the office. From then till dawn I dreamed up and rehearsed all manner of wild schemes to take me out of this dangerous situation. Or was it all perhaps just imagination? A Haldorian Trontar should never be guilty of an excess of that quality. But I made sure when the Senior Trontar sneaked in a bit before the regular opening time, that I was just, apparently, completing the last page of the report. The impression I hoped to convey was that I had spent the entire night in working and worrying.

"It's okay," the Senior Trontar growled after he had studied the completed report. "Guess you can take a couple of days off, Ruxt. I believe in taking care of my men. Say," he asked casually, "I suppose you didn't understand those figures you were working up, did you?"

"No," I said, "I didn't pay any attention to them, they were just something to copy, that's all." I felt confident that I could out-fence the Senior Trontar any time at this little game, but what had he and the Adjutant been whispering about before they had come in?

"But you used to be a statistician, didn't you?" He looked at the far corner of the room and smiled slightly. "But you take a couple days off, Ruxt. Maybe we'll find something good for you when you come back." He smiled again. "Don't forget to check out with the Locator before you go, though. We don't want to lose you."

I stumbled home, not even noticing the hate-filled glances my armor and blue skin drew from the natives along the streets. The glances were standard, but this feeling of being doomed was new.

They were going to get me. I felt sure of that, even though my Sike Test Scores had always been as low as any normal's. But how could a Haldorian disappear on this planet? Aside from skin color, there was the need to keep body temperatures at a livable level. The body armor unit was good only for about a week. Find a surgeon/replacer and bribe him to change me to an Earthman? I saw now how ridiculous such an idea was. But was there nothing but to wait passively while the Senior Trontar and the Adjutant, and whoever else did the dirty work, all got together and railroaded me off?

Haldorians, though, never surrender—or so the Mil Prop lad would have us believe. Right from the time you are four years old and you start seeing the legendary founders of Haldoria—Bordt and Smordt—fighting off the fierce six-legged carnivores, you are told never to give up. "Where there's Haldor, there's Hope!" "There's always another stone for the wolves, if you but look." I must confess I'd snickered (way deep inside, naturally) at these exhortations ever since I'd reached the age of thinking, but now all these childhood admonitions came rushing back to give me strength, quite as they were intended to do. I found that I could but go down like any Haldorian, fighting to the last.

IV

So I put on my dress uniform the next day, and made sure that nothing could be deader than the dulled bits, or brighter than the polished ones. A bit of this effort was wasted since I arrived at Headquarters looking something less than sharp. The cooling unit in my armor was acting up a bit; and, also, three Terran city guerillas had tried to ambush me on the way. You take quite a jolt from a land mine, even with armor set on maximum. Some of those people never knew when they were licked. No wonder their Spanglt Resistance Quotient was close to the highest on record.

I got through the three lines of guards and protective force fields all right, checking my rayer here, my armor there—the usual dull procedure. By the time I reached the Admissions Officer I was down to uniform and medals.

"You want to see the Accountant?" the Admissions Officer asked incredulously. "You mean one of his staff! Well, where's your request slip, Trontar?"

"I've come on my own, Sir," I said, "not from my office, so I haven't a request slip."

"Come on your own? What's your unit? Give me your ID card!"

Let's see, I thought, I've abstracted classified material from the files and carried it outside the office, I've broken the chain of command and communication, and, worst of all, I'd tried to see a senior officer without a request slip. Yeah, maybe I'd be lucky to end up as a *live* deckhand on a space freighter.

A bored young Zankor with the rarely-seen balance insignia of the Accountant's Office rose from behind the Admissions Officer.

"I'll take responsibility for this man," he said casually to the A.O. "Follow me, Trontar. I was wondering when you'd turn up."

"Me?"

"Well, someone like you. Though usually it's scared sub-clerks that we drag up. And that reminds me." He turned to another young and equally bored Zankor standing nearby. "Take over, Smit, will you? They're bringing in that sub-clerk who's been writing those anonymous letters. I've reserved the Inquisition Room for a couple of hours for him."

I followed the Zankor as he strode away, wondering as I did if they had more than one Inquisition Room.

He led me into a small room just off the corridor and motioned me to a chair. "Before you see the Accountant, Trontar," he said, "I'll have to screen what you have. It may be that we won't have to bother the Accountant at all."

The smooth way the Zankor talked and his friendly manner almost convinced me that we should both put the interests of the Accountant first. But then it occurred to me that a man with the gold knot of a Zankor on his collar wasn't often friendly with a mere Trontar. That thought snapped me out of it and I knew I should only give the minimums.

"I've got documents," I said—"document" is such a lovely strong word, "which prove that the official report on the invasion and occupation of this planet is false." That, I thought, was as minimum as one could get.

"Ah, and have you?" The Zankor still looked bored. "Well, let's see them, Trontar," he said briskly.

The Zankor had that sincere look the upper class always uses when they are about to do you dirt. They blush that heavy shade of blue, almost purple, and they look you straight in the eye, and they quiver a bit as to voice ... and the next thing you know, you're shafted.

"I'm sorry, Sir," I said, "but what I have is so important that I can give it to the Accountant only."

He stared at me for rather a long moment, pondering, no doubt, the pleasures of witnessing a full-dress military flogging. Then he shrugged and picked up the speaker beside him. He didn't call the Trontar of the Guard to come and take my documents by force. I could tell that even though he spoke in High Haldorian, that harsh language the upper class are so proud of preserving as a relic from the days of the early conquerors. No, he was speaking to a superior—there's never any doubt as to who is on top when people are speaking High Haldorian—and then I caught the emphatic negative connected with the present-day Haldorian phrases meaning Phase II and Phase III, Terraforming. So even though I don't know High Haldorian, and would never be so incautious as to admit it if I did, I knew roughly what had been said.

And I was frantically revising my plans.

"Follow me," the Zankor said, after completing the call. "We'll see the Accountant now, and—" he looked at me sincerely—"you'd better have something very good indeed. You really had, Trontar."

The Accountant turned out to be a tall and thin Full Marshal, the first I'd seen. He was dressed in a uniform subtly different from the regulation, and he wore only one tiny ribbon, which I didn't recognize. He had the slightly deeper-blue skin you often see on the upper classes, though this impression may have been due to the green furnishings of the room. It was, in fact, called the Green Room, when the Terrans had used it as one of their regional capitals.

I saluted the Accountant with my best salute, the kind you lift like it was sugar and drop as if it were the other. The Accountant responded with one of those negligent waves that tell you the saluter was a survivor of the best and bloodiest private military school in existence.

"Proceed, Trontar," the Accountant said, leaning back and relaxing as if he didn't have a care in the universe.

I launched into my speech, the one I'd been mentally rehearsing. I told him I knew I was breaking the chain of communication, but that I was doing it for the service and for Haldoria, etc. Any old serviceman knows the routine. I was, as I ran through this speech, just as sincere and just as earnestly interested in the good of Haldoria as any Haldorian combat Trontar could be. But, deep inside me, the old Ameet Ruxt was both marveling at the change in himself and cynically appreciating the performance.

The Accountant interrupted the performance about halfway through. "Yes, yes, Trontar," he said brusquely, "I think we can assume your action is for the good of Haldoria, may the Empire increase and the Emperor live forever. Yes. But you say you have material dealing with the overall report on our invasion and occupation of this planet. You further say this material shows discrepancies in the official report—which you imply you have seen."

"Yes, Sir," I said, and I handed over the several sheets of paper which comprised the old report and the changes of the new. Meanwhile, behind me, the Zankor was invisible but I had not a doubt but that he was there, keeping the regulation distance from me.

These people knew their business.

The Accountant took the collection of papers and compared them with some others he had on his desk. I continued to stand at Full Brace. Once you've been chewed out for slipping into an Ease position without being so ordered, you never forget.

The Accountant laid down the papers, scanned my face, got up and walked to the far end of the room. In front of a mirror he stopped and fingered that one small ribbon, quite, I thought, as if he were matching it with another one.

He came back quickly and sat down again. "Zankor," he said, "set up a meeting with the top brass for this afternoon. I'll talk with the Trontar privately."

The Zankor saluted and was on his way out the door when the Accountant spoke again. "And Zankor...."

"Yes, Sir?"

"I should be very unhappy if the top brass here—the *present* top brass—found out about this material the Trontar brought."

The Zankor swallowed hard and assured the Accountant that he understood ... "Sir."

Then we were alone and the Accountant was suddenly a kindly old man who invited me to sit down and relax. I did. I really let go and stretched out, I forgot everything I'd ever been taught as a child or had learned on my climb to the status of Trontar. I relaxed and he had me.

I had been caught on the standard Haldorian Soft/Hard Tactic.

"Disabuse your mind, Trontar," the Accountant snapped, and he was no longer a kindly old man but a thin-lipped Haldorian snapper, "of any idea that you have saved the Empire—or any such nonsense!" Having cracked his verbal whip about my shoulders he just crouched there, glaring at me, his mouth entirely vanished and his eyes—well, I'd just as soon not think about some things.

Yes, and then he gave me the Shout/Silence treatment, the whole thing so masterfully timed that at the end he could have signed me on as a permanent latrine keeper on a spy satellite in the Slug Galaxy. A genius, that man was. The sort of man who could—and probably did—control forty wives without a weapon.

"Your information, as it happens," he said after I had regained my senses, "checks with other data I've received. It might be, of course, that the whole thing is a fabrication of my enemies. In that case, Trontar—" he looked at me earnestly—"you can be assured you'll not be around to rejoice at or to profit from my downfall."

"Of course, Sir," I said, quite as earnestly as he.

"But we both know that you are only a genuine patriot," he said with a hearty chuckle, a chuckle exactly like that of a Father Goodness—that kindly old godfather who brings such nice presents to every Haldorian child until they are six, and who on that last exciting visit brings, and enthusiastically uses, a bundle of large and heavy whips to demonstrate that no one can be trusted. Efficient teachers, the Haldorians.

"Just a genuine patriot," the Accountant repeated, "who has rendered a considerable service to the Empire. Trontar," he said, all friendly and intimate, "the Empire likes to reward well its faithful sons. What would you most like to have or to do?"

"To serve Haldoria, Sir!" I was back on my mental feet at last.

He dropped his act then. He was, I think, just practicing anyway. We had a short talk then, the kind in which one person is quickly and efficiently pumped of everything he knows. After about ten minutes of question and answers, the Accountant leaned back and studied my face carefully.

"Have you considered Officers' Selection Course, Trontar? I might be able to help you a little in getting in."

Officers' Selection Course was, I knew, Fighter Basic Course multiplied in length and casualties. Less than 20 per cent graduate ... or escape.

"No, Sir," I said. "I wondered if I mightn't be of more value to Haldoria in some way other than being in the combat services." So now I'd said it and there was nothing to do but to go on. "Perhaps," I ventured, "I might be of some help in the administrative services."

The Accountant said nothing, his face was immobile, his hands still. He'd learned his lessons well, once.

"In fact," I said, deciding to go for broke, "with my knowledge of the language and the customs here, I might be of most service to Haldoria right here on this planet."

"Had you guessed, by any chance, Trontar," the Accountant's voice was neutrally soft, "that we won't be terraforming this world? And that we may not even exploit the slavery proposition?"

"I thought both those possibilities likely," I admitted.

"But you know that in such a case we would have no administrative services on this world? Thus you are, in fact, asking for a position that wouldn't exist." The Accountant, without a change of position or expression, somehow gave the impression of looming over me.

"I thought," I said, trying to pick exactly the right words, and at the same time all too conscious of a twitching muscle in my left eyelid, "that there might be an analogous position, even so."

The Accountant loomed higher.

"If only," he said, "you hadn't come to us, Trontar. I mean that you, in effect, sold your associates out to me. And I hold that once a seller, always a seller. If I could be certain that you are and will be perfectly loyal to the Haldorian Way...."

I managed to quiet the twitching eyelid and to look perfectly loyal to the Haldorian Way.

"Yes, Trontar," the Accountant said decisively, "I'll buy it."

———

The results of my conference with the Accountant were not long in appearing.

The Haldorian troops were called in, along with the military governors and the whole administrative body, and they all shipped out, somewhere into the Big Out-There they all love so much. A surprised Earth was informed that she was now a full-fledged and self-governing member of the Haldorian Empire. The Terrans were not informed of the economic factors behind this decision, though it might have been cheering for them to know that their Spanglt Resistance Quotient indicated they would make unsatisfactory slaves. Nor did the high cost of terraforming the planet get mentioned. We Haldorians prefer the gratitude of others towards us to be unalloyed with baser, or calculating, emotions.

Not all the Haldorian personnel went out to fight or to administer. I understand the space-freighter run to the battle fleet in the Slug Galaxy gained many new deck-hands, among them one whose uniform showed the marks where Trontar's stripes had perched.

As for myself?

Well, a relatively minor operation changed me into a black-skinned Terran, though the surgeon/replacers could do nothing, ironically enough in view of my new color, to increase my resistance to heat. I remember those stirring days of combat sometimes, usually when I am making my semi-annual flight between Churchill, Manitoba, and Tierra Del Fuego. In fact, during those flights when I am practically alone is the only time I have to reflect or remember, because on both of my estates there is nothing but noise, children, and wives.

But it's a good life when the snow is driving down out of a low gray overcast, just like it does back on Haldor. It's a good life being Resident Trader on Terra, especially when one is, on the side, a trusted agent of the Accountant. It would be a perfect life—if the Accountant hadn't been right about people being unable to stop selling out.

Right now I'm up to my neck in this Terran conspiracy to revolt against the very light bonds Haldoria left on this planet. But how could I resist the tempting offer the Terrans made me? The long sought-for good life, it now occurs to me, isn't so much in escaping from something, but in knowing when to stop. But that I know. I'm drawing the line right now. I'll just tell that agent of the Slug Galaxy that I have no intention of selling out both this solar system *and* Haldoria!